Animals in My Backyard
RABBITS
Pamela McDowell

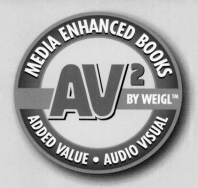

MEDIA ENHANCED BOOKS
AV²
BY WEIGL™
ADDED VALUE • AUDIO VISUAL

Go to **www.av2books.com**, and enter this book's unique code.

BOOK CODE

F736049

AV² by Weigl brings you media enhanced books that support active learning.

AV² provides enriched content that supplements and complements this book. Weigl's AV² books strive to create inspired learning and engage young minds in a total learning experience.

Your AV² Media Enhanced books come alive with...

Audio
Listen to sections of the book read aloud.

Video
Watch informative video clips.

Embedded Weblinks
Gain additional information for research.

Try This!
Complete activities and hands-on experiments.

Key Words
Study vocabulary, and complete a matching word activity.

Quizzes
Test your knowledge.

Slide Show
View images and captions, and prepare a presentation.

...and much, much more!

Published by AV² by Weigl.
350 5th Avenue, 59th Floor New York, NY 10118
Website: www.av2books.com www.weigl.com

Library of Congress Cataloging-in-Publication Data

McDowell, Pamela.
  Rabbits / Pamela McDowell.
     p. cm. -- (Animals in my backyard)
  Includes index.
  ISBN 978-1-61913-269-6 (hard cover : alk. paper) -- ISBN 978-1-61913-273-3 (soft cover : alk. paper)
  1. Rabbits--Juvenile literature. I. Title.
  QL737.L32M44 2013
  599.32--dc23
                              2011050304

Printed in the United States of America in North Mankato, Minnesota
1 2 3 4 5 6 7 8 9 0 16 15 14 13 12

022012
WEP020212

Project Coordinator: Aaron Carr   Art Director: Terry Paulhus

Weigl acknowledges Getty Images as the primary image supplier for this title.

Animals in My Backyard

RABBITS

CONTENTS

Meet the rabbit.

She has long ears. She is about the same size as a cat.

She lives with her family when she is young.

When she is young, she hides in the nest from other animals.

She hears well with her long ears.

With her long ears, she knows when danger is near.

She eats plants with her big front teeth.

With her big front teeth, she also cleans her fur.

She can see with her large eyes.

With her large eyes, she can see all around her at the same time.

She can move fast with her long legs.

With her long legs, she can jump, hop, and kick.

15

She comes out of the nest at night.

At night, she can find food without being seen.

She may live in the city.

In the city, there are good things to eat.

If you meet the rabbit,
she may be afraid.
Do not run after her.

If you meet the rabbit,
stay away.

RABBIT FACTS

These pages provide more detail about the interesting facts found in the book. They are intended to be used by adults as a learning support to help young readers round out their knowledge of each animal featured in the Animals in My Backyard series.

Pages 4–5

Rabbits have long ears. There are 28 types of rabbit. Rabbits can be found in forests, grasslands, wetlands, and deserts. More than half of the world's rabbits live in North America. A rabbit's fur can be brown or gray, and it may turn white during winter. These colors help the rabbit blend into its surroundings to hide from predators.

Pages 6–7

Rabbits live with their families when they are young. Young rabbits are called kittens or kits. A kit can easily fit in a person's hand. Kits are born without hair and cannot open their eyes for their first 10 days. The mother rabbit stays away from the nest to avoid attracting predators. She will visit her kits only once each day to feed them.

Pages 8–9

Rabbits can hear well with their large ears. They can turn their ears in all directions to listen for predators. When a rabbit is relaxing, its ears lay down along its back. If there is noise or any sign of danger, the rabbit's ears will stand up and turn toward the sound. A rabbit's predators include hawks, owls, foxes, raccoons, dogs, and cats.

Pages 10–11

Rabbits have big front teeth. They use these teeth to chew grass, leaves, clover, and flowers. In winter, rabbits gnaw on bark and twigs for food. This also helps to wear down their teeth. A rabbit's teeth will grow about 4 inches (10 centimeters) each year. This means their teeth grow almost as fast as human hair.

Rabbits use their large eyes to see in all directions at once. A rabbit's eyes are on each side of its head. This allows the rabbit to see almost 360 degrees. With such a wide field of vision, a rabbit can watch a hawk approaching from behind and above while looking for a safe place to hide to the front or side.

Rabbits can run, hop, and kick with their legs. They protect themselves by hiding or running very fast. A rabbit that is chased will zigzag quickly and even swim to avoid a predator. It can run up to 18 miles (29 kilometers) per hour. Its powerful back legs can kick a predator or thump the ground to warn other rabbits of danger.

Rabbits come out of their nests at night. Rabbits hide in their nests or dens during the day and come out at night to eat. In the dark, rabbits can see eight times better than humans. A den can be 10 feet (3 meters) deep. To make a den, the rabbit will dig with its front feet and push the dirt out of the den with its back feet.

Rabbits may live in cities. Rabbits live close to open spaces, such as fields and meadows. Many rabbits have adapted to live near humans, however. Rabbits that live in or near cities often eat vegetables, grass, and flowers. A gardener may need to build a fence more than 2 feet (60 cm) high to keep rabbits out.

Rabbits are often found in parks and natural areas. In the spring, people may discover a nest of baby rabbits that seems abandoned. It is important to remember that the mother rabbit does not stay with her babies. She is probably close by. Do not disturb the nest. The mother will return at night to feed her kits.

WORD LIST

Research has shown that as much as 65 percent of all written material published in English is made up of 300 words. These 300 words cannot be taught using pictures or learned by sounding them out. They must be recognized by sight. This book contains 60 common sight words to help young readers improve their reading fluency and comprehension. This book also teaches young readers several important content words. These words are paired with pictures to aid in learning and improve understanding.

Page	Sight Words First Appearance
4	the
5	a, about, as, has, is, long, same, she
6	animals, family, from, her, in, lives, other, when, with, young
8	hears, well
9	knows, near
10	big, eats, plants
11	also
12	can, eyes, large, see
13	all, around, at, time
14	move
15	and
16	being, comes, find, food, night, of, out, without
18	city, may
19	are, good, there, things, to
20	after, away, be, do, if, not, run, you

Page	Content Words First Appearance
4	rabbit
5	cat, ears, size
6	nest
9	danger
10	teeth
11	fur
14	legs

Check out av2books.com for activities, videos, audio clips, and more!

1 Go to av2books.com

2 Enter book code   F 7 3 6 0 4 9

3 Fuel your imagination online!

www.av2books.com